This book belongs to

....

but I'm happy to share it!

For Johnny and Ronnie,
and for Chloe, Oliver and Ben, for sharing.

CATERPILLAR BOOKS
1 The Coda Centre,
189 Munster Road, London SW6 6AW
First published in Great Britain 2013
Text and illustrations copyright © Sally Anne Garland 2013
All rights reserved
ISBN: 978-1-84857-368-0
Printed in China
CPB/1800/0251/0113
1 3 5 7 9 10 8 6 4 2

Share

Sally Anne Garland

This morning I got up, ready to play –

Mum said, "Your **cousin** is coming today.

He's only little, so show him you care."

"Please remember,
it's important to **share**."

As soon as
he came,
he wanted
my bear.

Mum said,
"Remember, please
let him share!"

Poking and **P u l l i n g** him,
poor little Ted!

So I went to play…

...with my
dolls instead.

But he was behind me –
he followed me there!

Mum said, "He wants to play,
please let him **share**."

Jumping and bumping,

he bounced on my bed.
I gave up doing that and...

...played dress-up instead.

He followed me,
wanting to see
what I'd wear.

Mum said, "He's having fun, please let him **share**."

Grasping

and

grabbing,

my

beads fell

and

s p r e a d .

I gave up doing that and...

...read my book instead.

He was there in a flash,
as I chose Princess Clare.
Mum said, "He wants to see,
please let him share."

Jostling and jiggling around as I read,

I gave up doing that and . . .

...watched TV instead.

He followed me in
and started to stare.

Mum said, "He likes it,
please let him
share."

Bobbing and blocking
my view with his head,

I gave up doing that and...

...did painting instead.

He followed me again
and climbed on a chair.
Mum said, "He's copying,
please let him share."

Scribbling

and

scrawling -

"My picture!" I said.

I gave up doing that and...

...had lunch instead.

He ran in the kitchen and reached for my pear.

Mum said, "He's hungry,
please let him
share."

He grabbed at my plate

and it fell

to the floor.

Huffing
and
puffing,
I walked out the door!

I asked, " When's he going?
I've had enough!"

Mum said, "Try to be patient –
I know that it's tough."

"All that he wants is to be
just like you.
That's why he copies
whatever you do!"

When Auntie arrived
she saw my despair.

"Just wait," she said,
"Now it's *his* turn to share."

Hugging and
squeezing me,

"Thank you,"
he said.

Then he was gone...

...and I sort of **missed** him instead.